Medusa N' Rio

By

Eddie J Martin

Janice, Dorothy, and Jesse...the team is back in town.

Medusa

He screamed when he saw "IT." He kept on screaming until his heart gave out and he died right there where he lay. He was never touched by Medusa, and she was mad because she wanted to at least cut his throat with one of her long fingernails. Maybe, she could still do that. The blood should be still running through his body, and she could drink from the opening in his throat.

 Sometimes things don't go like they should. It had taken her a few minutes to reach the apartment and she really wanted to make do with the time. It was too late now to go for another victim.

Medusa was a monster, a gorgon. She was described as having the face of a hideous human female with living venomous snakes in place of hair. Glazing directly on her, would turn onlookers to stone. Sometimes, Willow felt like and looked like a gorgon. That is when it came out, and she just had to kill somebody, anybody.

Confession

Janice Willow cannot remember when it first started happening to her. Back when she was a kid, she thinks maybe even before that; she would wake up in the middle of the night. The next thing she recalls is that she would be on the other side of town in her nightclothes with blood on her hands. She never knew how she got there. One way or another, she got back home without anyone knowing she had left. Her feet would be dirty, and blood all over her.

She would take a shower, and she remembered her mother saying something about why she was taking a shower early in the morning. She would always say she felt like she had ants crawling all over her body, and she just had to get that feeling off her. After that, every so often something like every few months, that feeling would come over her. The same thing would happen except then she would read the newspaper or hear her parents talking about another killing that had happened that night. It took a while before she realized she was that killer. She went to the therapist. She never told her what was wrong, but she said that something truly was wrong with her, and then she would mention to her what had happen. The therapist felt that she should tell the authorities and Janice felt that this wouldn't be good at all. A few nights later, she changed into the medusa and visited the therapist. The next day, it was in the newspaper that the therapist had been murdered by some type of animal, they believed.

Many incidents after that, she went into the military with many killings following her. She was contacted by the CIA, and they informed her that they knew what she was doing. They did not want to put her in jail, but wanted her to do what she was doing all the time for them. There was no option, and that is where her career with the CIA began.

Dorothy Malone

38 years old and black

5 foot, 10 inches

135 pounds

Measurements to drool for.

While Dorothy was in the military, she killed her X boyfriend's girlfriend. She received life imprisonment for that. The CIA heard of her and what she could do. They hired her and made her an offer she could not refuse. She took them up on it right away. She had been in prison for two years up until then. She still had her looks and shape. She felt now was a good time to disembark from the feds if she was offered the chance. She was, and they did. If she completed a job they had for her, then she would gain her freedom. The only stipulation was that she may not make it through the assignment alive. "What the hell!" Dorothy thought, "At least I'll be out of here."

After that assignment there were a few others. She liked the job, the pay, and travel. She stayed on.

Jesse Bo-T

Age-26

Ht-5'8

Wt-165

Jesse was a drug smuggler AWOL from the military. The CIA, Interpol and other organizations around the world had been looking for him for the last five years with no success. Jesse knew about the underworld, and how to get around in it. His only Achilles heel was his mother. When he heard that she had passed away, he needed and wanted to go to the funeral. On his way getting off the plane, which is when they picked him up, and that is when they made him the offer. If he were to do this job for them, they would forgive and forget the charges. If not, then he was looking at 25 years in prison. He had 24 hours to make up his mind. They would accompany him to the funeral. Jesse wasn't a dumb man and he figured there was some way. Regardless of how much time they gave him, he wouldn't do it. There was some way he could get out and they gave it to him, and he took it. Once they took the cuffs off him, he was out of there, but then there was the catch. They informed him that he could never get away from them. They would always know where he was. Once that happened, everything was off the table and he would go straight to jail... There was always a catch.

Once the assignment was over, they asked him whether he wanted to extend his contract. It didn't take Jesse long to tell them "hell no." He was getting out of Dodge, and he never wanted to see them again. The only ones that he would probably miss were the two women he worked with, Janice Willow and Dorothy Malone, two fine ******* but the hell with that. He would see them again in another life, another time, or another place.

CHAPTER 1

Agent stone walked into his boss's office (agent Jenkins). "I think we just about got it together," Stone said, "I just need to contact Janice."

"Do you know where she is?" agent Jenkins asked.

"We always know where she is. Stone says it is the other two that we have problems with. Once we get in touch with Janice, then she'll know where the other two are. I don't know about Dorothy, but Jesse will love Rio, that is if he's not on his high horse again. But I do believe if Janice calls, he'll respond."

"What about Dorothy?" Jenkins asked.

"Well, you know since she has that money, she may not want to go, but I don't think money is the only thing that moves her. It is that excitement."

"Whatever you have to do to get them on the job, do it," Jenkins said, "This job is a must, and as soon as we can get it taken care of, we have to do it."

"I'll contact Janice ASAP," Stone said.

****

Janice Willow was sitting on the patio of a very excusive hotel in Berlin, Germany having breakfast, O.J., coffee, toast, and bacon. She knew she should stay off the bacon because it would put too many pounds on her. At 28 and 5:10 125 pounds, she was getting up there and she didn't need all that, but she still had it. I doubt if anyone would throw her out of bed except for that small problem she had, and no one needed to know about that. She was 20 stories high and she could look over the balcony and see the people below; of course they all looked like ants, but it was a nice view. Maybe sometime tonight, she'll get out and check out the party life. She had been in Berlin for about a week now after completing a job in Vietnam. That one was quick and easy, and only a couple of people got dead. Maybe she'll get the chance to stay in Germany for couple more days before the next assignment, she hoped so anyway. She was about to grab a piece of that bacon when the call came. She looked at the phone and saw it was agent stone. I guess that waiting for the next assignment was just that, wishful thinking; after the third ring, she answered.

"This is Janice," she said.

"Agent stone here. Janice, how's it going?"

"Oh, so so," Janice said.

"You ready to go back to work?" Stone asked.

"Not really, but I won't turn it down," Janice said. "Where to this time?"

"How would you like to go to Rio de Janeiro?" Stone asked.

"Well, I've never been there before, and I hear they have some beautiful scenery there."

"That's true Janice, everyone should get to Rio at least once in their life. By the way Janice, do you think you could get a hold of Dorothy and Jesse?"

"You mean you don't know where they are? You found me pretty easily."

"You are different Janice. You know that we thought if we asked you, you could find them a little easier than we could. We know you know where they are."

"I could find them; it may take a couple of days," Janice said.

"Find them and get together with them, and tell them what the assignment is. This will be right up Jesse's alley. If we ask Jesse, he probably won't want to go for us, but we know he'll do anything for you."

"I wouldn't be too sure about that. The last time he was very hesitant, but then when you mention Rio that may change his mind. Give me a couple of days. And as far as Dorothy since she's got that money, she's been traveling all over the world. She has her own plane now you know, but I do have a private number for her."

"Do you want to tell me about the assignment?"

"I'll tell you that when you get to Rio. Let me know when you have everyone together."

CHAPTER 2

30,000 feet in the air in a Lear jet, Dorothy Malone was sitting with her legs stretched out. On the opposite side of her, rubbing her feet, was a toy boy. That is what she called them, after all, this was the second or third one since that last assignment she was on. I don't know what to do, she thought. Since she got that money from her Deceased husband, she had been living it up, but she was getting kind of old she thought. The only time she got to feel alive was when she was out with Janice and Jesse on one of their assignments from the agency. Since then it had been toy boy after toy boy.

This one was about 23 years old, white, and blonde headed. He had a body like a bodybuilder. She came to find out that those guys with bodies like that are not all they are made out to be. Oh, they are good in bed for a minute and then all they do is look at their self in the mirror. She even caught one once kissing himself, what's with that? I'm right here, maybe it's something wrong with me, she thought. She looked down at herself and saw the firm breasts, flat stomach, and long dark legs which were still firm. Oh no, she thought, it's not me, I still got it. At least this guy was good for rubbing her feet, but she was afraid that she would be sending him back to where she picked him up pretty damn soon.

Janice just called a little while ago about a meeting in Rio de Janeiro to meet Jesse. I know it'll be exciting; it always is when Janice calls.

She informed the pilot to change directions from Sydney, Australia to Rio, Brazil.

****

Jesse had just finished having sex with a young Swedish girl of about 18 when the phone Rang. It was Janice Willow.

He thought at first not to answer, but he knew she would just keep calling.

"Janice, how in the hell do you manage to find me wherever I am. Have you got some kind of locator on me or something? I even changed my phone."

"Nothing like that Jesse," she said, "I just have a feeling for you wherever you are, and I love you, you know that Jesse."

"Yeah, yeah just tell me anything Janice. What the hell do you want this time? I'm kind of busy. I got myself a job working real hard trying to make a dollar; you know how that is."

"Don't lie to me Jesse, I'll bet you have a little honey right there in bed beside you right now. Is that the second or third for the day?"

"Now, there you go Janice, getting into my business. I haven't had sex in …a while now."

"How would you like to go to Rio de Janeiro?" Janice asked, "They got plenty of ladies there."

"Rio de Janeiro!" Jesse exclaimed, "You mean chocolate city? Paradise and a half***** ***** I may go for that. What's the job like?"

"I don't know right off Jesse, but as soon as we get there, we'll learn that then."

The young girl that was beside Jessie grabbed at his ***** and he slapped her hand.

"What was that?" Janice asked.

"Oh, that was nothing, but I got to go. Call me back and tell me everything I need to know, and about my transportation. You do have transportation for me, don't you?"

"Don't worry about that Jesse, everything will be taken care of."

****

CHAPTER 3

Hotel Rio was on the main thoroughfare; that is where Janice, Dorothy and Jesse stayed. Janice was in room 222, Dorothy in room 523, and Jesse was in 1526. All were on different floors, but they contacted each other by Lou of the cell phones.

Agent stone was due to meet up with them two days after they got there in room 523. Once there, agent stone started briefing them about their assignment.

****

Rio was booming at the time. It would put New Orleans Mardi Gras to shame, and Jesse had been there a number of times. It was like he was in a candy store. He didn't know which one to grab first. There were all kinds of colors and flavors; this was for him. He did not know why he was just getting to Rio. After all he had been everywhere else, but he would have to watch himself. He couldn't afford to overindulge. He was known to do that. There was a time that he had sex so much until he couldn't walk and had to lay up for two weeks. He almost died just lying there watching all the pretties walk by; he won't do that again. His limit would be no more than 3 a day. One woman passed by and she looked just like an Angel. He wouldn't mind having her there and then. However, there was another one looking better than her. He changed his mind about the first one, and thought he would love to have the second one and then there was a third. No, no, he needed to keep his mind on the job he was sent to do and leave all these pretties for another time like maybe... tonight. After all, agent Stone wouldn't be there for another two days.

****

The Castle was 20 miles north of Rio on a high mountain top looking down on the Atlantic Ocean. Inside the Castle, sitting at an oblong table were five people. There were four men and one woman. The man sitting at the head of the table was a Pakistani of about 65 years of age. He had a pot belly which was resting on the table. He had a balding head with one diamond earring in his left ear. He wore a white shirt which was open at the collar. They called him the Baron.

To his left was an Asian man of about 5-foot 2, clean shaven head, a green and yellow short sleeve shirt, and diamond rings on all his fingers. They called him Tock. To his left was a black man, 5'8 approximately 170 pounds. He had a mustache, but no eyebrows. He had a low haircut, and they called him chess. To his left was a Creole man of about 5'10 and 150 pounds. He wore a three-piece suit. His head was full of white hair. He appeared to be about 35 years old. They called him Mandre. To Mandres left, was another man of European Descent. He spoke five different languages, and he was 42 years old. He wore a sport outfit of mostly Caribbean colors. His name was Angel. Next to Angel was a beautiful Asian girl, 6 feet tall 100 and 15 pounds. She had a pair of lips that you would want to Make Love to. Her name was Starlet.

Each person had their specialty, but all were killers. The Baron was the overall boss. They weren't just any killers, they were worldwide killers. A call would come in for a job to be done from all over the world, depending on what type of job the Baron would send that person. The girl was something special. She was more of a medusa that changed with a type of toxic drink that would transform her to this thing. She was used for special jobs. Once given this potion, it would last for a number of hours and then she would change back after she had murdered the subject. The Baron had his chemist work on that potion four years before he got perfection. During the meeting, the Baron gave a folder to his crew, and in that folder was the subject that they were to eliminate. It was placed in front of them and they were told not to open it until they left. They knew the protocol because they had done it many times before. No one knew of the other's assignment. Each one had a drink in front of them, just one drink. They finished the drinks after going over the minutes from the last meeting. They all got up and departed. They never worried about their wages because it was always deposited in their bank accounts.

The Baron held one of the men back so that he could chastise him. The last hit he had the target didn't die right away, but lingered for a few hours. That just wouldn't do, you never know what the person could tell in that length of time. He hoped he wouldn't have to bring it to chess' attention again.

This was the meeting that agent Stone had with the team. All 5 of the hit men and women had to be illuminated including the Baron. Wherever they had to follow these people to do the job, they had permission to do it. It was up to them to figure out how, where, and when.

Agent stone had told them where most of these people hung out. What remained was just how they were going to arrange who would go after who. So, they cut it down like this:

Jesse would go after chess. He hung out at the beach, and not just any beach, but a nude beach. Chess was known to be a little freaky. If he killed him in record time, then he was to go after madras. They would have to see on that one.

Dorothy was to go after pinky, he was a club man. You could always find him at the Angel club buying everyone drinks.

Janice was to go after the Baron, and if she founded within her means, also go after Scarlet (the Medusa).

CHAPTER 4

Regardless of whoever got finished first with their hit would find the others and help them. It seemed like the right thing to do.

****

Janice received a call from agent Stone.

"The Baron is having a cocktail party tonight, and you have an invitation."

"So, things have changed now?"

"It happens that way. You know that I'm sure you'll get to know the baron. A car will be around to pick you up, say 10pm, and Janice, use what you got to get what we need."

Dorothy walked into the Angel club at 11:00 o'clock, grabbed her a seat at the bar, and spotted pinky right off. He also spotted her. It was love at first sight at least for pinky. It didn't take him long to make it over to Dorothy and start a conversation. He offered to buy her a drink which she accepted. An hour after they met, he wanted to take her somewhere else. He knew the town very well and they started from there. 3:00 o'clock that morning, they had made it back to his place which was a penthouse in the better part of town. She hadn't planned on it, but they ended up in bed. That was the quickest that had ever happened to her and the same with him. Well, so much for leading him on.

Pinky, she found was an excellent lover and he talked all the

15

way through the lovemaking. What's with that? But he was saying some nice things as she liked that. Maybe he will just put it on like a woman does a man, but she didn't think so, she played along. It's all in the game. The next morning, they woke up making love and after breakfast, he took her shopping. He really knew the town and especially all the nice places to buy what a girl likes. She came back with so many packages that they needed help taking them up to his penthouse. She didn't know it, but he had departed from her and went to a jewelry store. He pulled out a small package, opened it up and pulled out a chain bracelet with all types of doo-dads on it. She had a couple like it, more exquisite really, but she played the part and acted like it was new to her. He put it on her wrist. She kissed him and made a big deal out of it; he liked that.

A couple of days later at dinner, he told her that he had to go out of town on business. It would take him a few days, but he surely didn't want to be away from her that long. So he thought to himself for a minute and asked her whether she would like to accompany him.

"I don't know," she said "I've only just gotten here in Rio and really haven't seen that much of it. Where are you going?"

"Argentina," he said. "You'll love it."

She informed the team and agent Stone and told them with any luck, she would be coming back alone.

At 10: PM, Janice was picked up by an automobile just as they said she would. She was taken to the Castle, 20 miles away. It was a long ride but the automobile she was in made a ride a lot easier being a limousine Mercedes. Once there, the driver drove to the front of the building under the orchards and the door was opened by a doorman. Before they got to the entrance, there were other cars ahead of them with women getting out looking almost as good as Janice, but that was hard to do. Janice had worn a stunning outfit and even the other ladies were looking at her as she entered the building. There was one or two other black women in the Castle. There was a European and an African. The Baron was at the door greeting everyone and shaking their hands. When Janice got up to him and took her hand, he looked at her. It was more of a stare and he held her hand longer than he did the others.

"Maybe you could honor my invitation for dance later on," the Baron said, "I sure would love that."

"I'd be honored," Janice said.

There must have been close to 200 people in the room. Janice had a little problem getting around everyone, but once they looked at her and saw her attire, most moved out her way and stared at her. A waiter came over to her with a champagne tray and she took one. The waiter asked her to come with him, he would find a place for her to sit. The Baron would be over as soon as he could get away. She followed the waiter, and he took her to a sitting area that no one had set in. It seemed as if it was waiting for someone. She figured out later that everyone knew it was the Baron's private sitting place. She sat down, crossed her legs with a large portion of it showing, and set back. By looking over the contour of the room, she saw what looked like duchesses, prentices, and people that were of high esteem. The women looked excellent and the men were gorgeous, Rio, I should have been here years ago.

****

CHAPTER 5

Tock had stayed at the beach close to midnight. He left with two scrunches female and Jesse was right behind him. They went to some small bungalow and Jesse found a way to look through a back window since it was on the 1st floor. They all had a few drinks together and started undressing. They listened to music and played with one another. "God damn," he said, "That should have been me, but no, I'm out here a peeping Tom when I should be in there with them. I don't know if I can handle this," he thought. Maybe, if they drank enough, he could do him right here. The next thing he knew the doorbell rang and two more pretties came into place, and they started taking off their clothes. "Oh, hell no," he thought "This is getting to be too much. He is not going to have sex with all these women I just know that" (although he knew he could do it). The next thing that Jesse saw was Tock sitting over in a lounge chair with a tall glass of champagne. He watched the ladies having sex with each other and started playing with him.

"What the hell is going on?" he thought. He was letting the pretties waste away while he just watched. So, for the next two hours, he just watched. His peter was harder than a locomotive, and for a while there, he could barely stand up. After the two hour's, the girls put on their clothes. Tock walked over to each one, paid them, and they left. Then he went into the shower and stayed about 10 to 15 minutes. He came out and went to bed. Jesse sat down on the ground and took in what he had just seen. "This can't be for real," he thought. He had never seen anything like it. That's not what you use a good woman for. He wondered whether he had been missing something.

On the other hand, there's no better time than the present you can't ask for anything better than this. He unlocked the window and crawled through. He made it to Tock's bed. He was in there laying on his back, and Jesse took out his switchblade and put it on Tock's throat. He woke up and his eyes went wide. Jesse pushed and held it there with two hands. He twisted it and pulled it out. Tock was bleeding heavily on his pillow, otherwise he just shivered and squirmed. Jesse cleaned his knife on the sheet and put it in his pocket. He went to the front door, looked out and confirmed there was no one around. He started to leave, thought about it, went back and picked up the fifth of Scotch that he had seen earlier. Tock wouldn't need it.

****

Starlet was at the Baron's affair. Her hit was in there, and she was cozying up to him. He was in to voodoo, and scarlet had persuaded him to go out into the countryside for an outing. They were to have the outing that night and they took off in the middle of the affair. 20 miles outside of the Castle was where the affair was to be. People were all gathered around in a circle with a voodoo priestess there. She had a Python wrapped around her. The group started chatting and ranking a kind of drank that Starlet's friend wasn't aware of. As the gatherings got further into the night and the dancing and the witch doctor parading one thing or another, Starlet and her friend were taken to a cabin. They were to spend some time in the cabin. At that moment, Starlet took a drink of her potion, and she and her friend started to Make Love. An hour or so later, starlet started to change. Her friend had fallen asleep. The Medusa started coming out in her and she couldn't control it. Other than that, it was the way it was supposed to happen.

The medusa was a monster, a gorgon. Having the face of a hideous human female with living venomous snakes in place of hair. Gazing directly on her would turn some onlookers to stone. Eyes turned to slits, mouth turned up, and teeth extruding out like a werewolf. Her body changed to one never seen on a human, and her hair moved around like snakes. Her large breasts disappeared, the beauty that was once there was gone. The only thing that resembled the old Starlet was gone, and that is when her friend woke up. Upon viewing her, he screamed. The village people heard the scream and all noise stopped. The dance stopped, the music paused, the voodoo priestess stopped what she was doing, and it seemed like the snake stopped its movements.

 At dawn, Starlet came out of the jungles dressed only in her panties. All the villagers had retired for the night. She found some of the village women's cloths, put them on, and went into the cabin. Her friend's body had been moved and was nowhere in sight. She got into the car and drove back to the Castle and to her room. No one asked about her friend; they thought that he had gone back to town.

CHAPTER 6

Earlier, the Baron and Janice were getting along fabulously. They seemed to have a lot of things in common, and he liked that. Later on at night, he asked her whether she wanted to spend the night since there was a room she could occupy. There was no need to go back to town. She told him she hadn't brought any clothes with her and that she would have to go back to her suite at the hotel to get her cloths. He told her that she would not have to do such a thing. He could send someone to town to pick up her things, and she agreed. The room that he put her in was larger than the one she had at the hotel, and she was very surprised at that. He made no attempt to sleep with her. It seemed that he only wanted to be with her and that would suffice, maybe for him, but not for her as far as getting close to him to kill him. A little earlier, she had seen the girl named Starlet leave with this guy during the evening, and she never saw them come back.

At 2:00 in the morning she was escorted to her room where she retired. The Baron and Janice danced a few times, but the rest of the time was spent talking. A few people came by the area, and he introduced her to them. She has to admit that it was a nice evening.

The next morning, Janice woke up to breakfast in bed. It was coffee, toast, OJ eggs, bacon, ham, and mushrooms. Her clothes from the hotel had been brought over and laid on a couch in the room. She dressed up and went down the stairs to meet the Baron. After a few minutes of conversation, he wanted to take her on a tour in the countryside to show her his property. For the rest of the day, they drove around and at one point had lunch at a resort.

Once during the trip, she thought she saw someone following them and she informed him.

"Oh yeah, that's a couple of my men," the Baron said, "They follow me everywhere."

That would be nice to know. She thought she would have to tell agent Stone about that, but then again knowing him he already knew.

CHAPTER 7

Dorothy and pinky had made it to Argentina. They spent a couple nights dancing and dining, and just having a real good time. A few nights after that, he went out but didn't say where. So, she figured he was just doing his job and she wasn't sent to monitor that. Whoever he was there to contract on, that was his business. If she had a chance to do him before that, then she would have. Otherwise she would just take care of her business. One night, he came back and said that they could go back to Rio the next day if there were no place else she wanted to see. She told him there were maybe a couple of other places they could see. She hoped he could put off leaving for a couple more days. He said he could, and the next day, they went touring again around the city and into the mountains. They came across a deep ravine overlooking a Valley, and she wanted to stop and check that out. They came up on a Cliff that looked down and saw that it was very deep. At the bottom was a bunch of boulders and trees. If you were not careful, you would slip and fall and that would be the end of you; they even had signs telling you to be careful. Dorothy and pinky went up to the edge of the ravine and looked down. She pretended that she was afraid and turned around and started walking back up towards the road. Pinky stayed where he was looking over the cliff. In one quick move, Dorothy turned around and pushed pinky over the cliff, he screamed all the way down.

Dorothy called agent Stone and reported to him that the 'P' was down. She was headed back to Rio.

Chess had $100 bill that he had rolled up to sniff cocaine that was on a nearby table. He was not supposed to mess with drugs. He had made a contract with the Baron, but the Baron just didn't know how good this stuff was. For the last couple of years, he had been on the stuff and doing rather good except for that miss he had on that last assignment. The Baron would not tolerate that. He would either fire him or take another action. This next assignment had to be straight and no misses. A ballplayer in the USA? He had never been there before, that should be a nice trip for him, a nice vacation. He thought maybe he could make it at least a week's trip. He took the hit of cocaine, laid back and thought about it. Houston TX. November it shouldn't be too bad he heard it does get hot in Texas, and he couldn't stand the heat. The word was that the best time to hit this ball player would be in his hotel room. He liked the women, and each player had their own room.

Days later, he was in Houston. The team was already there practicing. Since he had a little time to spare, he dived right into his favorite sport, cocaine. The first time around, he got antsy. He was on the stuff and started it. The kill he had missed before could be blamed on the cocaine, but no one wanted to hear it especially the Baron. He had already gotten paid for the hit, and he knew the Baron. He had to make this hit or not go back too Rio. The Baron's team was supposed to be the best around. There was no mistakes as far as the Baron was concerned, so, it was said. And the pay was damn good. There was one choice, that he had either stop the business or stop the cocaine. He didn't see how he would ever be able to stop the cocaine, and he needed the money to buy the cocaine. He would have to try one more time and hoped the Baron won't hear about it.

Chess made it back to Rio after a successful contract. He spoke to the Baron about it and said that he had had no problems. The Baron appreciated that he had a successful hit. He told Chess that he could stay at the Castle that night because there were some things he wanted to talk over with him. So, the Baron put him on the third floor along with scarlet. That night, Chess drank a little more than he was used to and went to bed early. Earlier that night, he had seen Janice and commented on what a fine woman she was, and wished he had seen her first.

That night, after he had fallen asleep, someone entered his room. It was the medusa.

CHAPTER 8

The Baron summoned Starlet to his office and told her that the Tock was dead and that he was trying to locate the ones who did it. He wanted her to take care of the situation.

He said, "We can't have that done to our people, unless we do it ourselves. In a couple of days, we should know who this person is. Go down there and handle it the way you always have. I'll let you know, are there any questions?"

A couple of nights later, Starlet was in the Tangiers bar. That is where he was, Jesse Bo-T or something like that. She thought that it didn't matter; she would get to him in no time. Jesse saw Stella and thought that there were fine girls in Rio, but not as this girl. He knew right off that he had to have her. He asked her for a dance, and it started from there. After his ******** he knew she couldn't refuse that. He had her prime ready to go. Right after midnight, they were in bed together making love. Stella went in the bathroom and took her tonic and went back to bed. In the meantime, Jesse went out of the room to get some ice from the cooler. While out there, he met another young lady finer than Stella and they got to talking. Being Jesse, and greedy as he was, he was trying to talk her into sex and Being the ********** he was, she agreed. Meanwhile back in the room, Starlet had made her transformation into the medusa. Jesse would be back in a minute, and she was ready to rip his heart out, but he never came back. He was one floor below having sex with the little pretty he had found.

The medusa waited as long as she could and went out looking for someone else to kill. She found a young boy of about 18, one floor above going into his room. She came up behind him, pushed him into his room and began to cut his throat and mutilate him. An hour later, she went back down to her room and went to bed. At dawn, Jesse came back in the room and got in bed.

At first light, Starlet woke up, looked at Jesse and saw he was still alive. The first thing Jesse did was to grab her and Make love to her. There was one thing about the tonic, you could only use it once every other day. So, she was out of luck for two more days unless she found another way to kill him.

On that second day, Jesse went out to the store and while out there, he found another honey that he wanted to Make Love to. He never made it back to the room where Starlet was. She knew one thing for sure, Jesse Bo-T was nothing but a whore monger. He loved making love more than she did.

The Baron and Janice came back from dinner one night and he told her why not sleep in his bed that night. It had been three to four nights and they had not slept together. She asked whether that was what he really wanted. He responded that he thought it was about that time.

"All the help are off for tonight, and I gave my men the night off. This would be the perfect time."

That was the same thing Janice was thinking, what a better time than this. They both undressed and got into bed. She thought that since this was the first and last time, she should let him taste a little bit and then she thought again, oh hell no, none of this he'll ever get.

Once in the bed, she made an excuse to go back to the bathroom. When she came back, there was a small derringer in her hand and she pointed it at the Baron.

He looked at her and spoke, "You've got to be shitting me?"

"No," Janice said, "this is where you get off."

There were only two rounds in the derringer. She shot him twice in the head, there was nothing like making sure.

Once back at her hotel, she called agent Stone and told him that the Baron was no more. She asked him, "Who's left?"

He responded, "We've been looking for Mandre after his trip to the states, but he made some mistakes there. We are grateful the Baron had him eliminated. Of course we found no body. So, it seems like the only one left is Starlet."

CHAPTER 9

The team met in Dorothy's room. They were discussing their episodes and Janice said the only one left was Starlet, and she described her.

"You've got to be kidding me," Jesse said, "that sounds like the girl that I was with the other night."

As Janice described her further, Jesse said, "Yes, that's the girl!"

"You one lucky *** Jesse," Janice said, "She's one stone killer."

"You think you could find her again Jesse?"

"I don't know, I didn't find her the first time, she found me."

"Then the Baron had a hit on you, I'm sure of that," Janice said, "If he sent Stella after you."

"We'll have to find her," Dorothy said, "Do you think she went back to the Castle?"

"I don't know," Janice said, "but I can't go back there. It would have to be you Jesse."

"What about that hotel room we were in the other night, do you think she might still be there?" Jesse asked.

"I wouldn't think so," Janice said, "That would be one stupid move. Why don't we check it out?"

The Baron was found the next morning by the maid. They called up the two bodyguards and informed them of the death. One was a heavyset Russian with a thick mustache and short body, the other was a Filipino somewhat taller than the Russian.

"We didn't do such a good job," the Russian said." His name was Phillip.

"Don't seem like it," the Filipino said. His name was Sinclair.

"You think the girl got to him?" Sinclair asked.

"Who else?" Phillip responded. "She's the only one that got that close to him. Sometimes, he was overly cautious of her, but I guess he wasn't cautious enough. What you wanna do?" Phillip said.

"After all he was our boss. Yeah, and there goes a paycheck," Sinclair said.

"We could try running the operation ourselves, but the Baron had all the information. We wouldn't know where to start. We know that he gets a call once a month about who to hit and for how much, but that's about all. We have no Contacts. First of all, maybe we should find this girl and take her out of action, and then we could concentrate on what's next. What about Starlet you think she knows something?"

"I don't think so Phillip, she is just a worker like us."

"First of all, I think we need to get rid of this body. The same place we took Mandre would be a good spot, he'll never be found there. There'll be other people looking for him wanting a contract, what do we tell them?"

"We don't have to tell them nothing, we not the boss."

"You know," Sinclair said, "we could take some of those jobs ourselves. There was a lot of money going around."

"I know," Phillip said, "but to tell the truth, we not really that good. The people that the Baron had were professionals."

"What the hell you think we are?" Sinclair said, "We just didn't get off the turnip truck."

"Let's talk about it later," Phillip said, "I'm getting a headache."

CHAPTER 10

Starlet was told by Phillip and Sinclair what had happened to the Baron. They deliberated on what they were supposed to do since the outfit was disbanded. They wondered who will take over.

"I guess that will be up to me now," Starlet said, "I know everything about the business and where the bodies are buried (so to speak)."

"Well, we do too," said Sinclair, "we buried the bodies."

"Who do you think killed the Baron?" Starlet asked.

"It can't be no other than the woman he had staying here," Phillip said, "She waited her chance and took it. We need to take care of her, we can't have the word going around about what she did."

"Phillip and I were going to do that as soon as we find out where she's located."

"No," said Starlet, "I want to take care of that myself, whether you know it or not. The Baron and I was really close. Get the word out where she's at I'll take it from there.

Is there any disagreement about me taking over and you two going out into the field? After all, within a year on that job you'll have quite a bit of money, what you say?"

Phillip and Sinclair agreed to Starlet taking over the organization and the search was on for Janice Willow.

The search was also on for Starlet. Since no one wanted to go back to the Castle, they thought that they would wait for her to come back to town.

Starlet had found out that Janice Willow was in hotel Rio and she got a room there. She thought that she would take her potion that night. Around 2:00 in the morning would be a good time to go to her room. First, she would scare the hell out of her and then mutilate her like she did all the others. She would like that, and she was sure that the Barton would like that too. On the way to the hotel, Jesse spotted her and told the team.

Meanwhile, Janice had spotted Phillip and Sinclair outside the hotel and she knew that they had probably brought Starlet. So, the plan was for Dorothy and Jesse to take care of those two while she handled Starlet. They knew that all this would be happening after midnight, and that is what they planned for.

Agent Stone was told what was happening and he asked whether they need any help. They all said no for him to just stay out the way.

At the hotel Rio bar, Phillip and Sinclair waited for Starlet to finish her job, but that wouldn't be for another couple of hours. Jesse and Dorothy came in separately and she sat near them. Phillip started talking to Dorothy and thought that since he had time on his hand that he would try to get over on her. Jesse sat and watched both men, waiting for an opportunity to take one out or both, whatever. At approximately one in the morning, Sinclair went to the bathroom and Jesse was right behind him. Sinclair was at the urinal, Jesse waited for his chance and stabbed him in the back. He then cut his throat and put him in one of the stalls. He washed his hands and went back into the club. Phillip never knew that his partner was gone. A while later, Phillip and Dorothy went up to one of the rooms, but Phillip never came out. Two men were seen leaving out the back of the hotel carrying a large trunk.

CHAPTER 11

Three that morning, Starlet had made it into Janice suite. She was growling and leaking saliva from the mouth. Her teeth were extending from the mouth, the hair was long and stringy. She had no breathing, no eyebrows. She was bent over like an old person. Her legs had gotten skinny and the feet had gotten larger with 2-inch toenails. Her hands and fingernails had gotten longer, looking like a Wolf. She headed towards Janice bedroom, opened the door and saw someone underneath the covers. She eased over to the bed and pulled the covers off the person, and beneath it, she saw someone looking back exactly like her.

The same hair the same face with mouth large and drooling with no eyebrows, on her head were real snakes not like hers. The hands were long and skinny, and the fingernails were long and hard as steel. Once the covers were pulled back, her duplicate reached out and smacked her face leaving marks on her face. She swiped at her again and cut her around the neck. Medusa #1 (Janice) leapt up from the bed almost to the ceiling and came back down on #2's back. She screamed and fought back but number one was on her with no respect. #2 ran out the room and headed to the hallway, but number one was right behind her. Number one caught up to her, tackled her and started biting on her neck and blood started to ooze. #2 bit number one on her shoulder and left a mark that would be there for days to come. #2 managed to get up and made it to the stairwell and started leaping down four steps at a time. Number one was skipping the stairs six at a time and caught up with her again. The two were screaming like two fighting dogs. If you watched them, that's what it looked like. Number two managed to get up again and she headed for the basement. From the basement, #2 headed for the street where they were having the parade. Once they went out to the street, everyone there was in costume and they thought the two medusas' were the same. No one made a big thing of it, they continued fighting. Number one chased #2 across the street and number one was hit by a horseman. The horse reared up and went wild. Number 2 headed for the alley and number one was right behind her. In the alley, number two ran across Jesse Bo-T and he looked at her in astonishment. He pulled out his pistol and took a couple of shots at her. Number one was coming right behind and #2 knocked Jesse down. However, he recovered and took a couple of shots at her. "What the hell is going on?" He wondered "It must be a couple of people in costume, they bout to get their *****shot up."

After they passed the parade, they came to a bayou and had to crossover it. #2 fell in while crossing, and number one dived in after her and they went under. Number one was at the bottom and pulled #2 down with her and held her. Number one's hand slipped from number two's ankle and she was turned loose. She made it back to the other side of the Bayou, climbed up, and started running down the alleyway. Number one had made up her mind that she was going to kill this one thing that looked like her. Pretty soon, she was up on the other side and running after #2. She ran into a pack of dogs along the way, and the dogs attacked her. She had to fight them off, killing most of them, but she wasted time. As she battled the dogs, #1 caught up with her. The remaining dogs ran off with their tails between their legs, that's when number one caught up to her and they started fighting again. Number one bit off #2's foot at the ankle and started for the other. After a short while #2's potion started wearing thin and she started turning back into Starlet. Once she turned, she knew she was dead.

CHAPTER 12

A few days later in Jesse's room; Janice, Dorothy, Jesse, and agent Stone were going over the assignment that had just ended, and how it came out.

"It must have turned out fairly good," Jesse said, "Everyone's here is unharmed. I didn't even get shot this time. But I tell you that I saw the damn nest thing in the alley the other night. It scared the hell out of me. They looked like two damn Wolves. I took a shot at them, but I was so shook up I didn't hit either one." For the rest of my life, I don't want to see no **** like that ever again."

"I heard they found Starlet in an ally the other night," Dorothy said, "Her eyes we're both out, her tongue had been pulled out and someone had pulled her damn hair out, and they said one of her foot was bit off. Can you believe that?" Dorothy said, "I wonder what got hold of her. She was one beautiful girl."

"I don't think we will hear any more from Phillip and Sinclair, that should be the end of their operation," Janice said.

"Well, if there is nothing else, I'll be leaving this place in the morning," agent Stone said, "You all take care of yourselves, and I'll be talking to you."

When stone left, Jesse said, "I'm sure he will. I don't want to see his *** for the next 10 years, how 'bout you girls?"

"You know I have no choice," Janice said.

"I don't mind," said Dorothy, "the only way I get my excitement is with you guys. What do you want to do now? You know, I have got this plane that would take us anywhere in the world. How about, let's fly somewhere."

End

EPILOGUE

More Janice Willow and the team to come in the near future.

AFTERWORD

Don't forget to get your copy of Ruben Kane.

ACKNOWLEDGEMENT

My daughter Beth Angie Martin... Thanks for the encouagement and all you do.

ABOUT THE AUTHOR

Eddie J Martin

Retired US Air Force

BOOKS BY THIS AUTHOR

Assassin

UNTITLED

www.ingramcontent.com/pod-product-compliance
Lightning Source LLC
Chambersburg PA
CBHW070355130626
46556CB00007B/3175